A new SCARETOWN book is released every month. Sign up to the mailing list at www.scaretownbooks.com for access to exclusive deals on the newest releases.

Join the conversation at www.twitter.com/scaretownbooks

THE MIND CONTROL APP

L.A. Drake

CHAPTER ONE

"HOW DEEP DO you think it is, Toby?" Marla asked, peering into the black water. The surface rippled gently and a dead leaf sank out of sight.

"I don't know," I replied, shrugging my shoulders as I held the thick rope between my hands. "But I don't plan on finding out."

"What if you fall in?"

"I won't."

"But what if you do?"

"I won't," I grinned, taking a few steps back.

The pond behind the school was technically out of bounds during lunchtime, but we didn't care about that. It took months of convincing, but eventually, Marla came round to my way of thinking. She worried about everything. Every time I planned something cool, she would warn me against it, but I'd do it anyway. Afterwards, she'd agree that it was a good plan after all. That's how we worked.

This time, my idea was *clearly* brilliant. No one had ever done it before. I'd be a school legend if I could pull it off right under the teachers' noses. The plan was simple. I tied a rope to a tree that hung across the pond and I would swing all the way across to the other side. It was so far that most kids thought it was impossible. I'd have to jump the last part because the rope wasn't long enough.

The whole place was a nature reserve. That's what the school called it, anyway. Really, it was just a big patch of overgrown land that no one knew what to do with. Sometimes, we'd have science classes near the pond and the teacher would catch tadpoles in a jar for us to look at. It was cool the first time, but it got a bit boring after a while.

"Come on, Toby," Marla whispered. "Lunch will be over soon. We need to get back before anyone notices."

"Just give me a second," I mumbled with my tongue wedged in my cheek as I concentrated. The rope was thick and it was difficult to grip. I strode backwards and wedged it between my legs as Marla's phone beeped behind me.

"Who's that?" I asked, turning to her as she flicked the screen.

"It's just a Buzztap," she shrugged.

"A what?"

"A Buzztap. It's this new app everyone's talking about. Haven't you got it yet?"

"Nope, what's it do?"

"It's like a game," Marla replied. "Every time it buzzes, you have to tap the screen quicker than your friends. It's a race."

"A race?"

"Yeah, look," she said, thrusting the phone in my direction. "It can buzz at any time day or night and you can see how quickly all your friends tap. I just beat Marcus and Sarah by 12 milliseconds but Allie beat me."

"What happens if you're quickest?" I asked, wrapping my ankle around the rope.

"I don't know, I've never won, but I heard it plays a video that is so funny it made a kid pass out."

"That's ridiculous."

"It's what I heard," Marla shrugged. "You should download it."

"I'll do it later," I mumbled. "I haven't got time for that nonsense now. I need to make this swing. Are you ready to record? No one will believe me if it's not recorded."

"No-one will care either way…"

"Huh?"

"I said I'm pressing record now!"

"Okay," I grunted, gearing myself up. "This is gonna be awesome!"

The ground beneath me was dusty and dry. Clouds of mud wafted into the air as I rocked back on the soles of my feet and prepared myself mentally to make the jump. The water was still and dark. The faintest hint of bubbles popped on the surface from something lurking below.

The rope was coarse and wide. I rested the edge of my palm against a knot and pulled it tight. The branch above bowed and bent under my weight, but it was strong enough not to break. There was nothing left to do but start running.

I took a deep breath and pushed my feet hard into the ground. I could see Marla's outstretched hand filming me from the side as I sprinted towards the water's edge. I grinned at the thought of the whole school watching my triumph on their phones.

I sprinted as fast as I could. The black liquid rippled gently as stones kicked out from under my trainers and landed deep within the pond. I planted my right foot and thrust my left knee towards my chest as I tensed my arms and jumped.

I surged skywards before plummeting back towards the water. Thankfully, the rope took my weight and I rocketed through the air as it swung neatly on the branch above. It worked perfectly. My takeoff couldn't have gone any better. My school uniform rippled in the wind and my hair flopped back past my ears.

I hoped Marla was still recording because everything was going just as I'd planned. The far side was approaching fast. I squinted my eyes and focused all my efforts on the dismount. If I messed up, I'd fall straight back into the dark water below. I had to let go of the rope at the perfect moment and leap the last couple of meters.

The rope groaned and stretched between my fingers. I strained my entire body and fought to stay upright as my torso tipped backwards. I had the momentum, I had to make a move. I pulled hard and tensed my muscles.

The ground was so close I could almost touch it. I lifted my foot and stretched my leg. The rope swayed and sent me off balance as I jumped. I tumbled forwards. Everything seemed to go in slow motion. The black water reflected my wide eyes back up towards me as I left the safety of the rope behind.

I was almost there. I'd almost done it. I stretched my arms out in front of me as I sailed through the clear air. A thousand thoughts raced through my mind in less than half a second. I thought I was going to make it. I thought I was going to be a school legend.

A smile crept across my face, but it was too early. I'd celebrated too soon. I thought it was all going right, but it was about to go very, very wrong.

CHAPTER TWO

THE WIND BLEW strongly against my hot skin. The solid ground felt so close, yet so far. I thought I was going to make it, but something was wrong. My foot was still caught in the rope. The thick cord wrapped tightly around my skinny ankle and tugged me back.

My fingers scraped the mud as my body fell short of safety. The sound of Marla's scream was cut off as I splashed into the cold, dark water. I couldn't breathe. The shock of the freezing liquid made my muscles spasm. I thrashed my legs downwards to right myself as the water rushed over every part of me. I was completely submerged in the stinking pond. Everything went dark. I twisted, turned and kicked until I felt myself shooting towards the surface.

Cold air ran across my face as I gasped for breath. Stagnant water dripped from my ears and the sound of Marla's laughter came into focus. I turned to face her voice and found my bearings. Kicking fiercely, I swam towards her. I'd almost swung all the way across the pond, so I had to swim all the way back.

The water was freezing. My clothes were soaked and clung to my skin as I kicked furiously and propelled myself across the pond. My trousers stuck to my knees and my t-shirt shrank to my shoulders.

Marla was laughing. Her muffled wail rebounded off the trees and echoed all around us as I reached the bank. The last of the water that had been blocking my ears suddenly cleared and Marla's voice grew sharper.

I shot her a look and she tried to compose herself. She wiped her eyes and exhaled deeply.

"Need a hand?" she asked, before bursting into another fit of laughter.

"Get me out of here!"

Marla held out her arm and helped me clamber up the muddy bank. I leaned forwards and rested my hands on my knees as I tried to catch my breath. Pond water dripped from every part of me. Strands of algae swung from my hair as my entire body shivered.

"Mr Simon is going to kill you…" Marla said in a quivering voice. She was still trying to hold back her laughter. I looked up at her and puffed out my cheeks. She was right. Mr Simon was our head of year and, more importantly, our science teacher. He was the strictest teacher in the school and we had about 5 minutes before our next class with him started.

"What am I going to do?" I asked, holding out my soaking wet arms.

"Take off your jumper, ring it out and put this on." Marla held out a jacket she'd yanked out from her bag.

I peeled my school uniform up and over my head. It was completely soaked through. I bunched it in a ball and squeezed as much water out as I could before shoving it in my bag.

"Thanks," I said, smiling weakly for the first time since I'd fallen in the pond.

"Hopefully your trousers will dry out a bit before we get back. Maybe you should phone your brother and ask him to bring you some spare clothes?"

"My phone!" I hadn't thought about it before, but my phone had been in my pocket the whole time. I pulled it out and a torrent of dirty water came with it. "It's completely ruined!"

"Calm down," Marla said, softly. "Maybe it'll still work."

"It won't turn on," I screamed. "It won't do anything!"

"It's just a phone," she shrugged. "It's not the end of the world. Maybe we can fix it later, but we have to go, class is starting."

I shoved my phone in my bag and slung the whole thing over my shoulder. Marla's jacket was too small, but at least it was dry. The sleeves stopped a few centimetres short of my wrist and the buttons only just stretched across my chest to fasten. My trousers were still soaked and I could feel the water running down my legs as we trudged back towards the school.

We squeezed through a hole in the fence that was common knowledge among the students but, somehow, the teachers seemed not to know about. The field was emptying fast. Kids had stopped playing football and were waiting outside their classrooms. Even the naughty kids that hung out at the far end were making their way back.

Marla urged me to hurry up, but I resisted. The longer I took, the more time my clothes would have to dry. We were halfway across the courtyard when the bell rang and queues of kids started piling into the classrooms.

"They're a bit dryer now," I said, pinching the fabric of my trousers between two fingers.

"Yeah…" Marla agreed, unconvincingly. "No one will notice a thing."

All the other kids had entered the classroom and the door was swinging slowly shut as Marla held out her hand and caught it. She led the way and found her seat. I took a deep breath and followed. The noise was deafening, but it soon stopped.

Mr Simon wasn't at his desk and my classmates were joking and laughing with each other as I stepped through the door. A paper aeroplane flew across the room. Music blared from someone's phone at the back.

Then, one by one, they all turned to stare. Like robots, they stopped what they were doing and faced me. Their faces changed. Their expressions turned blank. The laughter ceased. Their smiles faded and the light left their eyes.

I froze.

Everyone in the room was silent and staring. Then, they stood up. In one movement, they rose. Together, their arms left their sides and their fingers pointed in my direction as they stepped towards me. They weren't kids anymore. They weren't even human.

CHAPTER THREE

THE WHOLE CLASS moved as one. They raised their arms and opened their mouths. I stumbled back and felt my shoulders hit the whiteboard. They were like zombies, not thinking and not speaking.

One broke from the ranks. Matt Jenkins. He stepped into the aisle next to his desk. His hair was long and his nose was crooked. He stared straight at me and shouted.

"WHAT IS THAT?"

I didn't know how to react. I clasped my chest and looked to Marla for help. Her eyes followed Matt's pointed finger.

"Toby," she whispered. "Your hair…"

I brushed my hand across my head and realised why they were all staring. A long, slimy trail of green weeds fell to the floor. It had been in my hair since I fell into the pond. I felt blood rushing to my cheeks. My temperature rose as I pursed my lips and slowly looked up from the disgusting green mass on the floor. For a second, the class was still in shock, but it didn't last long.

Everyone erupted into fits of deafening laughter as I frantically ran my fingers through my hair to rid it of any traces of pond life. Green and black streaks splashed onto the rough, grey carpet. My wet shoes left dark puddles and flecks of water flew from my trousers.

"What's going on here?" It was Mr Simon. His cold, snarling voice snaked into the room and his thin, boney body followed. "I know you're not making a mess in my classroom, are you Tobias?"

"No, Sir," I choked, turning on the spot and facing the teacher. "It's just I…"

"Because it looks like that's exactly what you're doing."

The entire class turned silent. I could feel their eyes burning into the side of my head as I froze on the spot. I didn't know what to do or say. Mr Simon was right, I *was* making a mess. I suddenly felt very foolish. I should never have come to class in wet clothes, I don't know what I was thinking.

"I'm sorry, Sir…"

"Don't apologise to me," he croaked. "Apologise to *them*."

Mr Simon lifted his slender finger and jerked his cracked nail towards the rest of the class. Their round, pale faces turned slowly from Mr Simon and faced me. My eyes were wide and my stomach churned.

"I'm sorry…"

"What's that?" Mr Simon barked. "I don't think they heard you at the back."

"I didn't hear him!" Matt Jenkins called. He was grinning from ear to ear. He could hear me perfectly, he just wanted my humiliation to continue for a bit longer. I glanced back at Mr Simon. He knew exactly what Matt was doing, but he went along with it. He raised his eyebrows and nodded his head for me to speak.

"I'm sorry for making a mess," I said, finally, in a loud and clear voice.

"Now, take a seat and stop wasting everyone's time. You kids will learn some discipline if it kills me," Mr Simon said as he slung his bag onto the floor behind his desk. His nose was wrinkled and his eyebrows were furrowed. If there was one thing Mr Simon liked, it was to moan about kids. "It's your generation," he continued. "No discipline, no common sense."

"Here we go again…" Marla whispered as I squelched into the seat next to her.

"With any luck," I grinned. "We can keep him rambling until home time."

"Remember that time someone asked how to wire a plug and he spent two hours explaining why our generation won't amount to anything?"

"Easiest afternoon ever."

"And that," Mr Simon continued. "Is why young people today don't deserve to own homes."

I rolled my eyes and leaned back in my chair. My trousers were almost completely dried out and I was starting to feel comfortable again. Mr Simon's lessons were boring, but they weren't hard. All we had to do for the rest of the afternoon was sit back and let him rant.

The sun was high in the sky so I swung my hips around to catch the warmth from the window. I could feel my trousers drying by the second. Things were

17

starting to look up, but then a hand rose from the pack in front of us.

It was Matt Jenkins. He just couldn't resist stirring up trouble. Mr Simon was halfway through telling us about how much weaker we were than his generation when he noticed Matt's palm waving.

"What is it, Jenkins?"

"If our generation is so lazy…"

"And dumb."

"If our generation is so lazy and dumb, how come we know how to turn a computer on and you don't?"

A ripple of suppressed laughter made its way around the class. I couldn't see Matt's face, but I could imagine it. His smug smile would be driving Mr Simon mad. Matt was the most irritating boy in school. He got sent out almost every lesson. He couldn't sit still and he never missed an opportunity to wind someone up. It was funny when it wasn't directed at me.

Mr Simon's face was bright red. His jaw jutted out to the side and his teeth ground together.

"Listen to me, Jenkins," the old man said, leaning closer to Matt's desk. "You're not the only one who knows how to use technology. Who do you think designed those phones you're using? Who do you think invented the first computer? I can tell you, it wasn't a kid like you."

"Was it you?" Matt replied. "Did you design them?"

"Well, no," Mr Simon snarled. "It wasn't me specifically."

A kid on my left clamped his hand over his mouth to stop himself from laughing. Matt was making Mr

Simon look silly. I wanted to laugh too, but I knew it wouldn't end well if Mr Simon's pride was hurt. He was exactly the sort of teacher to triple our homework for the week out of spite.

"I guess we do have a lot in common after all," Matt smirked. "Neither of us have invented anything. At least I know how to use them, though."

That was the last straw. The kid with his hand over his mouth couldn't contain himself any longer. He blurted out a laugh so raucous it made me jump. Other students followed and soon the whole class was laughing in Mr Simon's thin, red face. Only Marla and I managed to keep our composure.

Mr Simon straightened his boney spine and stood up tall. He stepped carefully back around his desk and scoured the faces of the kids in front of him. His mouth was closed. His lips bulged where his tongue ran across his yellow teeth.

"You'll see," he muttered quietly. "You'll all see…"

"He's gonna blow," I whispered. Marla's eyes were wide and confused. We'd never heard Mr Simon speak so quietly before. He'd screamed and shouted at us a million times, but this was different. His voice was low and menacing. We could barely hear him over the laughter.

"One day soon," he continued. "You'll all be sorry. There will be no more laughter. No more jokes. No more *kids*."

CHAPTER FOUR

MATT JENKINS AND the rest of the class laughed even harder than before. Even I started to crack a smile. I was confused, but it was funny. Mr Simon was talking like a crazy person. Marla just smiled and shook her head. We both thought he would start shouting soon and everything would return to normal, but he didn't. He just kept muttering to himself about the end of the world and wiping the laughter from kids' faces.

"I think we might've gone too far this time," Marla whispered.

I shrugged and turned back to Mr Simon. His face was even paler than normal. His eyebrows hung low over his dark eyes and his jaw jutted out at strange angles as he rambled on and on.

"I think you might be right," I replied. "But at least it means no one's laughing at me anymore."

Marla rolled her eyes and turned away. Mr Simon stood up straight, looked at us all one last time and stormed from the room. The class fell silent as the door slammed shut. No one knew how to react.

"Is he coming back?" asked a girl in the front row.

"Who cares?" Matt Jenkins shouted, getting to his feet and climbing onto his chair. "The classroom is ours!"

"We should probably tell someone," suggested a boy at the back.

"And miss out on this golden opportunity?" Matt replied from the top of the desk he'd now climbed onto. "Don't you get it? We can do whatever we like. We're free!"

Matt Jenkins jumped up and down on the table top and sent flecks of mud flying from his shoes each time he landed. The kids nearest to him backed away and soon he was on his own in the centre of the room, still jumping and still laughing.

His crazed cackle was high-pitched and piercing. He wasn't afraid of teachers in other classrooms hearing him. He wasn't afraid of anything. It seemed like he was in detention every single day, but he never changed.

"Should we do something?" Marla whispered.

"Like what?" I replied, reclining on my chair. "Let's just enjoy the show."

As if he heard me, Matt Jenkins let out another mighty roar as he spun wildly in a circle with his arms stretched out to the side. The shock seemed to wear off and the other kids began to laugh again. They left their seats and mingled in groups of three or four, chatting and laughing. I stayed at the back with Marla and watched it all unfold.

Then something strange happened.

All at once, everyone except me stopped what they were doing, paused for a second, before frantically reaching into their pockets. They moved as quickly as they could, they didn't speak or laugh, they just acted. Every single person in the room except me reached for their phones. Students everywhere fumbled clumsily and swiped hastily at their screens as their devices rumbled noisily.

My phone never buzzed, of course. I flipped it over in my hands and tried all the buttons, but it was still dead from the pond water.

It didn't last long, but the noise was intense. Then, one by one, the buzzing stopped and panicked faces looked up from their screens. The room fell silent as they waited for the results. Tensions ran high. Marla was quick, but so were many others. A bead of sweat fell from her brow as she scoured the room intently for signs that someone had beaten her to it.

We didn't have to wait long before Matt Jenkins screeched even louder than before.

"I did it!" he yelled. "I'm the quickest and you're all losers!" He jumped higher and higher on top of the desk until his messy hair scraped the ceiling. The table legs bounced and rattled. The floor thundered. "Look!" he continued, thrusting his phone in the face of anyone nearby. "I was the first to tap. I beat you all!"

I glanced at Marla's phone over her shoulder and saw that he was right. His name was written in bold at the top of the league table. Marla was third.

"Unlucky," I scoffed.

Marla shoved me in the arm and slotted her phone back into her pocket.

22

"I'll get it one of these days."

In the centre of the room, Matt started to sing.

"I'm the Buzztap champion! Champion. Champion. Champion!"

"What do you get?" a voice from the crowd called.

"Yeah, what's the prize?" another added, climbing the table to look at Matt's phone.

"You think I'm gonna share my prize with you?" he snorted, jerking his screen away and shoving the other guy to the floor.

"Come on, show us!"

"Yeah, show us!"

The crowd called out, but Matt Jenkins ignored their pleas. He wasn't interested. He didn't care what anyone thought, he was going to receive his prize alone. The table wobbled as he hopped down to the floor and skipped excitedly across the room holding his phone close to his chest so no one could see.

His grin spread from ear to ear as he barged through the other kids. He was taller and wider than everyone else so it didn't take him long to clear a path and make his way to the corner. With his back pressed against the wall, he kept his phone in front of his face.

There was no sound, from the phone or the kids. Everybody stood silently watching Matt as he waited for his prize. His wide, toothy grin still beamed from his face, but it didn't last.

His eyes flickered as the light from the screen shone brightly. A video started to play, but there was still no sound. The skin under Matt's eyes twitched as he focused on what he was seeing. His lips were still parted, but he was no longer smiling. Something had changed. Something was wrong. His eyebrows raised and his eyes grew wide. His jaw fell slack and his skin turned pale as all the colour drained from his terrified face.

CHAPTER FIVE

"MATT?" I CALLED, sliding my chair back and getting to my feet. Some of the other kids turned around, but Matt didn't flinch. "Are you okay? What is it?"

He didn't reply, but I could tell something was wrong. His expression was completely different. Matt was always smiling, always joking. I'd never seen him look so serious before and it freaked me out.

I pushed my way through the crowd. Most of them had lost interest and were making their way back to their seats. Eventually, a gap opened up and I could get closer to Matt. His eyes were wide open but they were unfocused. His head lolled slightly from side to side as he stood with his arms swinging loosely by his hips. His mouth fell open and a strange sound gurgled from his lips.

"Uh… I…"

"What is it, Matt?" I asked, gripping his shoulder. "What did you see?"

"That's enough!" Mr Simon yelled.

I hadn't heard him enter and his voice made me jump. We locked eyes for a second before I had to look away. A smirk spread across his face as he glanced at Matt.

"I think he's ill, Sir," I said, gesturing over my shoulder.

"Nonsense," Mr Simon scoffed. "Back to your seat, Jenkins. Now."

"Yes, Sir," Matt barked instantly.

"See?" Mr Simon quipped as Matt practically ran back to his desk and sat bolt upright in his chair. "It's about time you kids started showing me a bit more respect."

"I…"

"I don't want to hear anything more from you, Tobias. Back to your seat."

I scratched my head and screwed up my face as I squelched back through the desks. My trousers were still damp, but most of the water had dripped into my shoes. I stared at Matt as I passed. We weren't friends, far from it, but I thought he would still acknowledge me. I thought he would give me a nod or a smile or *something,* but he didn't even flinch.

Matt Jenkins, the naughtiest kid in school, stared straight ahead without blinking just as the teacher had instructed. I couldn't believe it and, by the look on Marla's face, neither could she. Even the other kids in the class were muttering to themselves.

"It must be a prank," Marla whispered as I slid my chair into place next to her. "I bet he's building up to something."

"I don't know," I muttered, using my hand to block my mouth from the teacher's sight. "He looked out of it."

"Just wait," she said, patting my leg and leaning back on her chair. "He's gonna explode any minute."

We both stared at the back of Matt's head as Mr Simon started to speak.

"Now that you've all settled down," the elderly teacher snarled. "It's time to make some changes."

"I don't like the sound of this," I whispered, furrowing my brow and glancing at Marla.

"First things first, there will be no talking. Ever." I instinctively looked at Matt. This was the time when he usually had something to say. He'd make a joke or blow a raspberry or something. For a second, Mr Simon looked at him too, but Matt didn't make a sound and the teacher continued. "Secondly, I will need some help around here. Mr Jenkins, how about you?"

"There's no way," I said under my breath. "There's no way Matt helps him."

"Look," Marla urged with a nod.

Matt stood up silently. Every pair of eyes focused on him as he stepped around his desk and tucked his chair neatly back underneath. We all wondered what he was planning, but he gave nothing away.

The excitement started to grow. I could feel the butterflies forming in my stomach as I anticipated his next move. It was going to be big. Matt had never resisted making a joke out of something for this long before. He was building up to something huge.

I nudged Marla in the arm as we watched Matt walk slowly towards the front of the class. His back was straight and his arms were flat by his side. He walked with his head held steady and he didn't look anywhere but forwards. He reached the front of the class and stopped a few centimetres from the wall with his nose almost touching the whiteboard.

A few giggles rippled around the room as Matt Jenkins stood staring at the wall. Mr Simon scoured the faces to see where the noise was coming from, but the laughter stopped as his beady eyes moved from pupil to pupil. Then he smirked, raised his hands and clapped.

A single, sharp slap sprung out from between his hands and Matt Jenkins, the class clown and the most rebellious kid in school, jumped into the air, spun in a circle and snapped his heels together like a soldier standing to attention.

A sharp bolt of air shot from my mouth as I gasped loudly. Mr Simon's eyes flicked in my direction, but he didn't turn his head. He smirked and continued staring at Matt as the student stood bolt upright in front of the class.

"Now," Mr Simon hissed. "March."

Before I had time to understand what the teacher was saying, Matt Jenkins lifted one leg high into the air and slammed it down in front of him. The other leg followed and he moved briskly through the aisle. His rigid arms swung like metronomes by his side and his eyes never drifted from their position as he stared straight ahead.

I tried to get his attention as he passed by, but it didn't work. He was too focused. His pale, emotionless face stayed the same. Mr Simon called for him to stop and turn as he reached the far wall and

Matt did exactly as he was told. My jaw dropped open as he marched back to the front of the room and stood to attention.

It was slowly dawning on me. It wasn't an act. It wasn't a prank. Matt Jenkins was being controlled.

CHAPTER SIX

I SCRATCHED MY head as Mr Simon dumped a pile of books into Matt's outstretched arms. The teacher clicked his fingers and Matt started to hand a book to each kid in the class.

"What the…" Marla whispered.

"How?" I asked, quietly.

Marla was as confused as I was. Neither of us could understand what we were seeing. Matt's heavy, robotic footsteps made their way closer to us and I tried again, unsuccessfully, to catch his eye. He whipped the books in our direction without stopping and without blinking.

"This is…" Marla started.

"Amazing!" I finished.

"Huh?"

"Don't you get it?" I asked.

"Get what?"

"We'll never have to put up with his stupid jokes again!"

"But don't you think it's a bit… *weird?*"

"I think it's great!" I said with a grin. "He won't laugh at me now, will he?"

The thought of Matt pointing at my wet hair came to my mind again. I could still feel the pond scum dripping down my ankles, but the embarrassment was much worse, and Matt started it all. He was the one who humiliated me when I entered the class. He was the one who made everyone laugh at my expense just as he had done so many times before. I didn't understand why he was suddenly behaving like a teacher's pet, but I didn't care. If it meant he wasn't like his old self, it was fine by me.

I sat back and watched Mr Simon direct Matt around the room. He made him hand out worksheets and collect books. He made him wipe the whiteboard and even sweep the floor. By the end of the class, it almost seemed normal. Kids held out their completed work without even looking up and Matt would collect it. Not once did his expression change. The whole time, his face was emotionless and rigid. He didn't blink, look to the side or hesitate once. He was completely focused on any task the teacher set.

When the bell rang, Matt Jenkins was the only one not to react. He stood passively behind Mr Simon like a security guard.

"The bell is for me," the teacher bellowed. "Not for you. Now, pack up your things and make your way out in a calm and orderly manner."

Other than Matt and Mr Simon, Marla and I were the last ones out. It was a sunny day and the light burned my eyes as we stepped out of the dingy classroom. It was home time and kids from all over the school brushed past en masse. There was barely any room to move, but I still stopped and waited.

"What are you doing?" Marla called.

"One second!" I yelled over the crowd.

A moment later, Matt swung the door open and Mr Simon ambled out. The old man looked up from his phone to smirk at me as he strode past. He was a head taller than the swarm of kids and I watched his grey hair disappear away into the distance. When I turned back around, Matt was still in the classroom. He stood completely still with his arms by his side and stared straight ahead.

I took a step closer. A kid from the year above barged past and sent me tripping forward, but I stayed on my feet as Matt started to move. His stiff legs swept in long, rigid strides and his straight arms shuffled forwards and back.

He walked in a straight line, stopped, turned and continued through the door. Every movement was robotic. He never blinked. He never smiled. He didn't even stop when I stepped in front of him. His shoes hit my shins and he kept walking as I called his name. I stumbled back and to the side as Matt ploughed straight past me and through the crowd of moving bodies. I turned to Marla. Her skin was pale, her eyes were wide and a bead of sweat dripped from her forehead. There was something she wasn't telling me.

CHAPTER SEVEN

"MR SIMON MUST have something on him," Marla said as we left school and climbed the steps to the top deck of the bus. Many other kids were already sitting down and putting on their headphones.

"Maybe he threatened to call his dad," I guessed, as we took a seat at the back and the bus started to rumble into action. "I heard Matt's dad is super strict. He used to be in the army."

"Maybe," Marla thought. "But what if there's something more to it?"

"Like what?"

An old lady near the front coughed and the tiny dog on her lap jumped in fright.

"I don't know…"

"You're overthinking things again, Marla. If Matt wants to be a teacher's pet now, so be it. It's better than the alternative, right?"

"I guess…"

"Anyway, he'll be back to his annoying self by tomorrow, I'm sure."

"Maybe you're right," Marla agreed. "It just so confusing. Wait…"

"What is it?" I asked, but I didn't need her to tell me. All the kids on the bus suddenly reached into their pockets. Bags fell to the floor and elbows jutted into ribs as they frantically reached for their phones in the cramped seats.

Buzztap had struck again and the race was on. Marla didn't even pretend to care about stopping our conversation dead as she raced to be the first to tap. She rapidly yanked her phone from her pocket, but her grip failed as she spun the screen around. The phone flipped into the air and dropped to the floor.

"Ah, man!" Marla called, looking up at the other kids who had clearly already tapped.

"Better luck next time," I shrugged, drawing smiley faces in the condensation on the window.

"Whatever."

"Who won?"

"Why do you care?"

"I don't, I'm just asking."

"Someone called Callum Minks," Marla said through gritted teeth. "I came 312th."

"I know Callum," I said. "Nice guy, bit strange. Real goofy laugh. He's in my maths class."

"Good for you."

"You really care about this thing, don't you?"

"No," Marla shrugged. "But I'd like to win at something, just once, you know?"

Before I had a chance to answer, something caught my attention. The bus had been stationary for a while. The windows were steamed up and the loose bolts in the seats rattled noisily. The stairs were at the front and we were at the back of the top deck. I heard footsteps climbing.

Tufts of hair bobbled and shifted as the school kids on the bus stretched their necks to see what was happening. The steps grew louder and heavier. The people at the front stood up and obstructed my view. I turned to Marla but she just shrugged.

Then, they all turned. Every school kid, even the old lady with the dog, got to their feet and turned to face me. Behind them, a torrent of other kids filed up the stairs. They turned towards us and started marching. Their faces were ashen and expressionless. Their arms were stiff. Their eyes were cold and dead, but they focused on me and me alone. Together they marched along the narrow aisle as I frantically and hopelessly looked for a way out. There were no fire exits, no open windows. No escape.

CHAPTER EIGHT

I GRIPPED THE rough fabric and squirmed further back against the seat. Sweat dripped from my head and my knees shook. Marla edged closer to me as the robotic people advanced along the bus. The old lady led the way. Her thin, wispy hair wafted around her craggy face.

I opened my mouth to yell. My throat was dry and my tongue felt large and heavy. I coughed and choked as the soulless army drew closer. The lady reached a boney arm in front of her face and pointed.

"Room for a little one, dear?"

"Huh?" I muttered.

"Someone's let off a stink bomb downstairs," she said softly. Her hard features seemed suddenly less scary. Her dog wagged its tail as she cradled it in her arms. "He doesn't bite, I promise. Mind if we sit here?"

"No, of course not," Marla answered for me.

I felt myself blushing as blood rushed to my cheeks. I forced a smile and shuffled over. The kids behind the old lady weren't emotionless, they were holding their breath while trying to get away from the stink bomb.

I squeezed up next to Marla and opened the tiny window by my head. Warm air rushed in and whirled around the back of the bus as dozens of people filled the seats around us. We were so close to each other that none of us felt comfortable talking. Anything we said would've been heard by everyone else.

The waft of rotten eggs occasionally drifted up from the bottom deck and blended in with the lingering stench of pond water on my clothes. The algae had dried to my skin and it was uncomfortable to move. Every time I shifted on my seat, I felt it crack and crumble.

When our stop arrived, we awkwardly shuffled past everyone around us. The old lady feigned a smile and her dog sniffed my legs as we made our way past them both and stepped out into the sunny street.

The thick, dusty fumes parted as the bus pulled away. Marla's house was to the left and mine was to the right. We nodded at each other and went our separate ways. I couldn't wait to get in, shower and change my clothes.

I shoved my key in the lock, let myself in and called out for Mum or Dad. No one answered, but I knew they were home. Their cars were on the drive and I could hear the washing machine rumbling. I called their names again, they still didn't respond but I could hear something else in the kitchen.

They weren't talking. They were doing something. A chair leg scraped against the floor. A cupboard slammed shut. Clothes rustled. I approached the door and turned the handle slowly.

"Oh hey," Dad said, barely looking up from his phone as he desperately tapped the screen.

"Sorry Toby," Mum added, flicking her finger across her tablet. "We're just playing this new game."

"I beat you!" Dad yelled. "1089th! You're down in the 2000s!"

"Wait," I said, screwing my nose up. "Are you playing Buzztap?"

"Yeah! Do you know it?"

"It's all around school."

"It's great fun," Mum smiled. "I'm getting a lot better, aren't I dear?"

"Yep," Dad replied. "A few more days and we'll be in the top 500!"

They burst out laughing together as I rolled my eyes and made my way back out of the kitchen and headed upstairs. I chucked my stinking clothes straight into the laundry bin and jumped into the shower.

It was cold at first, but I didn't care. I needed to get clean. My skin felt rough and slimy at the same time. I cranked the hot tap all the way to the right until the water started to heat up. Steam gathered on the windows as I scrubbed my legs and arms. The pond scum had got everywhere and the water at my feet ran black and green.

I grabbed a bottle from the side and squeezed a long trail of shampoo all over my hair. It foamed up as I scrubbed my scalp. The bubbles ran over my face so I clenched my eyes shut tight. Several minutes passed as I blindly tried to cleanse every part of my body.

Eventually, the suds started to clear and I rinsed my hair one last time before stepping out of the shower and onto the cold, tiled floor. The bubbles had gone, but the steam remained. I could barely see anything. I held my arms out straight and felt for my towel. It had been hanging on the radiator and was lovely and warm as I wrapped it around my waist. The clouds of water vapour were still thick and motionless when I saw something through the mist.

In the corner of the bathroom, two figures stood silently. I wiped the moisture from my eyes and tried to focus, but there was too much steam.

"Hello?" I asked. "Is someone there?" There was no answer. They still stood and stared. I took a step closer and the fog shifted. They were big and tall. Adults. I couldn't see their features, it was too steamy. "Mum?" I called. "Dad? Is that you? What are you doing in here?"

Again, they didn't answer. I took another step and saw more. Their arms were raised. They pointed at me. My mind raced as my heart thumped against my chest. It couldn't be my parents. They wouldn't scare me like that.

One of the figures lurched forwards and made me jump. I stumbled backwards and tripped. I rolled onto my back, crawled towards the door and pushed myself up. My parents wouldn't do this to me, not unless something had happened. Not unless they weren't thinking straight. Not unless they had lost their minds.

CHAPTER NINE

THE TWO FIGURES stood in the steam and watched me fumble crazily for the handle. I gripped it with the tip of my fingers and yanked. The hallway carpet rushed up to meet me as I fell through the door. I rolled onto my back again and waited for them to emerge.

"Mum?" I croaked. "Dad, please!"

"Yes?" Mum replied.

"What do you want, Toby?" Dad answered. The sound came from behind me. They were both downstairs but if they were in the kitchen, who was in the bathroom?

I spun back around to face the door as the steam billowed out through the opening. The mist slowly cleared and more things came into focus. The shower, the sink, the towel stands. Wait, towel stands? They were new. I'd never seen them before. They were tall and thin with arms protruding at strange angles to hang fresh towels from.

Slowly, it dawned on me. I hadn't seen Mum and Dad in the bathroom. I hadn't seen anyone. It was the towel stands covered by the steam. They were vaguely shaped like people and the water vapour from my shower had played tricks on my mind. I shook my head and laughed to myself as I climbed to my feet.

After dinner, I went straight to my room. It had been a long day and I needed to sleep. The sun had just set as I climbed into bed. The covers were fresh and felt cool on my newly cleaned skin. The embers of the day faded behind the houses across the street as I shut my eyes and let my body sink into the mattress.

I could hear the faint rumble of the television downstairs and the occasional burst of muted laughter, but everything else was silent. I didn't want to think about the day that had just occurred. I didn't want to relive my failed attempt at crossing the pond or the look on Matt's face as he marched up and down the aisle at the beck and call of our grumpy old teacher. I didn't want to think about those things, but they forced themselves into my mind nonetheless.

I tossed and turned in the darkness. I kicked the covers off and pulled them back up. I flipped my pillow and tried each side several times, but I couldn't get to sleep. My legs ached, my shoulders were sore and my mind was racing.

Hours passed and I still lay wide awake. The sound of the television faded. Dad's feet clunked past in the hall. I heard Mum click their door shut and hit the light. A few minutes later, the snoring started and I knew Dad was fast asleep. Mum probably was, too.

My brother was staying with friends, so I was the only one awake in the whole house. I rolled onto my side and stared through the open window. A cool breeze passed under a flickering streetlamp. The light sputtered and flashed before turning off completely.

The streetlights were on a timer. They switched off at midnight every night. The darkness didn't surprise me, but the noise did. It started quietly and got louder. Footsteps ricocheted around the street.

I sat up straight and listened carefully. It sounded like a lot of people. Dozens, maybe more. They were walking, but not quickly. The steps were in time with each other. It sounded like a marching army and, when I looked out the window, that's almost exactly what I saw.

Lines and lines of people filled the street. They walked next to each other in rows of four and moved at exactly the same pace. Their legs lifted at the same time and their arms swung uniformly in the same motion.

I scratched my head and leaned against the windowsill. It was cool, firm and very real. I grabbed my arm and pinched the skin. The jolt of pain confirmed I wasn't dreaming. There really was an army of people marching past my house at five past midnight on a weekday.

They weren't soldiers. They were normal people in normal clothes. I leaned further forwards for a better look and managed to pick out faces from the neighbourhood. The guy from the shop was walking on the far side of the group. Our old postman was nearer to me. I was considering whether to call out when I saw someone else.

Matt Jenkins.

He was in the middle of the pack, marching perfectly in time with everyone else. To his left was

Callum Minks from my maths class. Neither were smiling. Their faces were rigid, their arms swung by their sides and their straight legs shuttled briskly back and forth.

Then, as if they all had the same thought at the same time, they stopped. Their arms clamped to their sides and their legs stopped moving. Their heads, as one, slowly started to turn. I felt the colour drain from my cheeks as I realised what was happening. Dozens of deadpan faces turned to my window. Their eyes were wide and white. Their mouths stretched tight. My chest thumped as my heart leapt from my chest and a cold sweat erupted from my forehead.

The army of emotionless people turned to face me completely. Their legs lifted and they stepped forwards in one unified motion. The clap of feet on concrete echoed in the night air. I let go of the windowsill and backed away from the glass. I had to run. I had to hide.

I turned to flee, but my room was dark. I twisted and pushed off from the wall. I sprinted towards the door, but something stopped me. I crashed into it and fell back. It was large and solid. It was human, but it barely moved.

I looked up from the floor and saw an expressionless face staring back at me.

CHAPTER TEN

I NO LONGER cared about being quiet. I screamed loudly as the soulless being beared down on me. The rough carpet burned my palms as I scrambled away. I flipped over and tried to get to my feet, but I fell. I slid onto my back and kicked my legs out in a blind panic.

"Woah, calm down, Toby!"

I paused and slowly lowered my feet to take another look at the thing in front of me.

"Dad?" I asked. "What are you doing here? I thought you were a…"

"A what?" he said. "What is going on here? Why are you making so much noise?"

"I… the people. On the street." I leapt to my feet and tugged Dad by the sleeve of his dressing-gown. "Look, there's so many of them and they started coming towards me and…"

"So many of what?" Dad asked, pulling the open curtain back further and looking both ways down the road.

"The people," I snapped. "They're right here…"

Except, they weren't. The street was completely empty. I flung my upper body out the open window and leaned as far forwards as I could, but I couldn't see anyone. Dad's thick fingers yanked me back by my shoulder and I looked up at him for answers.

"You had a bad dream," Dad said. "Just jump back into bed, it's okay now."

"It wasn't a dream!" I shouted, louder than I'd planned. "It was real. They were there, I swear."

I could tell by the smile on his face that my dad didn't believe me. I brushed past him and ran from the room.

"Don't wake up your mother!" Dad yelled as I clattered down the stairs.

If the mindless army wasn't on the street, maybe they were already in the house. I spun around the bannister and skipped down the last two steps. The hallway was dark and empty. I slammed my palm against the light switch and headed towards the kitchen.

Dirty dishes were piled in the sink and the fridge hummed softly, but there were no people. They weren't in the living room either, or even the garden.

"I don't understand…" I whispered.

"Happy?" Dad asked. "Now, get back to bed before you wake up the entire neighbourhood. I mean it."

Dad used his serious voice so I knew there was no point arguing. I trudged back up the stairs and slunk into bed. I lay awake for a while and planned how I was going to question Matt and Callum as soon as I got to school the next morning, but then I shut my eyes and forced myself to relax by breathing deeply.

When I woke, the sun was breaking through the open curtains and I could hear the clatter of cutlery in the kitchen.

"Porridge?" Mum asked as I plodded down the stairs and wiped my bleary eyes.

"No thanks," I muttered. "I'm running late."

I grabbed a single slice of toast and rushed out the door with my backpack over my shoulder. Marla was waiting at the end of the road with her face buried in her phone.

"Top ten!" she squealed. "One of these days, I'll get first place."

"Are you still playing that stupid Buzztap thing?"

"It's not stupid, it's fun," she smirked. "You're just jealous because your phone is still broken."

"Whatever," I shrugged, but Marla was right. It felt bad not having a phone. I had taken it apart, wrapped it in a towel, and left it on top of a radiator to dry out, but I suspected it was beyond repair. Every so often, I'd tap my pocket out of habit and feel the same pang of disappointment when I realised it wasn't there.

I told Marla about what I'd seen from my window the previous night, but she didn't seem very interested. In fact, she barely looked up from her phone the whole time.

"It could buzz at any second, Toby!"

"Fascinating."

"You just don't *get it*."

Streams of other kids joined together as we approached the school gates from all directions. I tried to make conversation, but Marla was still focused on the game. It seemed like everyone was.

Everywhere I looked, people had their heads down as they stared at the tiny screens in their hands, waiting for the next buzz.

"I'll see you at breaktime," I said. "Marla?"

"Huh?" she moaned, reluctantly looking up from her phone. "Oh, yeah, cool. See ya."

We were in different sets for maths. Marla was in the top and I was in the bottom, so we had to split up for our first lesson of the day. Normally I didn't want to leave Marla, but she was so weirdly focused on her phone that I was almost glad for the change. I watched the top of her bowed head bob around the corner and out of sight without looking back.

As I turned around, I had to stop suddenly. I had almost walked straight into someone else and just narrowly avoided colliding with them head-on. Their face came within a centimetre of my own and I smelled their stale deodorant. I backed up and apologised profusely, but they didn't react.

It was a kid from the year above. I'd seen him joking around with his friends before, but now he wasn't laughing. He wasn't doing anything. His cold, pale eyes stared straight ahead. He didn't flinch until I stepped slowly to the side. As soon as the path was clear, he marched forwards without saying a word or even blinking.

The bell was about to ring for the first lesson. I shook my head and hurried down the corridor. The door was open, but some kids were still waiting outside. About a dozen students lined up in the hall.

"What's up?" I asked. "Why aren't you going in?" Normally, everyone just takes their seat and waits for the teacher. "Is there something wrong?" I paused for a second, but no one replied. They all stood and stared, unflinching and unmoving. I shuffled past and entered the room.

More kids were inside. Some leaning back in their chairs, some sitting on the tables, but they were all chatting normally. I breathed a sigh of relief as I found my seat and two seconds later Ms Orbison, our maths teacher, burst through the door.

A flutter of papers fell from her arms as she dragged her chair from under her desk with her foot. Her face was red and sweaty as she dropped her bag to the floor and exhaled deeply.

"Right," she said, hands on hips. "Take your books out and go to page… wait. Where is everybody?"

"They're in the hall, Miss," a girl in the front row replied, nodding towards the door.

Ms Orbison's face screwed up in confusion. She flattened out her shirt with her hand, turned and walked back towards the door. As she pulled the handle, the other students flooded in. They marched past the teacher as if they had been waiting for her permission to enter the whole time.

At the very front of the queue, I saw Callum Minks. I tried to catch his eye. I wanted to let him know that I saw him from my window, but he never looked at me. None of them did. They simply marched to their seats and sat down in perfect unison with each other.

Ms Orbison stood at the front of the class with her mouth wide open. Her head tilted to the side and her eyes narrowed. She glanced in my direction and I winced. We were thinking exactly the same thing: something very strange was going on.

CHAPTER ELEVEN

THE CLASS WAS eerily quiet. Half the students sat bolt upright and stared intently towards Ms Orbison. Her lip quivered as she glanced around the room. She was as confused as I was, but she tried to continue. She wiped her glistening brow and introduced the day's topic. Algebra.

I sighed and leaned back further on my chair until the plastic groaned under my weight. I hated maths, and algebra was the worst part of it. Instinctively, I reached into my pocket for my phone but, of course, it wasn't there.

The kid in front of me was sitting completely upright with both arms resting on the table. Like a dozen other students, he was paying full attention to the lesson in a way Ms Orbison had probably never experienced before.

I looked out of the window as the teacher droned on about how to solve equations. The sun was shifting in and out of thick clouds. The football pitches were empty. I wished I could be out there playing with my friends, but I couldn't. I was trapped in a lesson like every other kid I could see through the windows.

The school was shaped like a horseshoe and, from one side, you could see straight into the classrooms on the other. I'd never seen it look so calm. In every class, kids stared straight at the teacher with their arms lying flat on the tables.

Every room I looked into was the same. Half the kids were relaxing, reclining and barely paying attention and the other half sat like robots. Marla's class was no exception. I could see her twiddling her pen and leaning on her hand. Next to her, Adam Kupla was sitting with a straight back and wide, piercing eyes focused on their teacher.

I was mid-yawn when the first buzz happened. Half the class didn't react, but the other half did. They didn't care that we weren't allowed to use our phones in school. They reached into their pockets and frantically unlocked the vibrating screens. A cacophony of tapping followed. Within seconds of each other, kids around the school bashed their phones in an effort to be first. They all wanted to be the next Buzztap champion.

After two seconds of manic activity, there was silence. Ms Orbison was in shock. She didn't know how to react. I'd never seen her shout before, but it looked like she was about to if Sara hadn't done it first.

"Second place!" she screamed from the front row. "Pipped to the post by Eloise Gretchen. Just my luck!"

Sara slumped back down into her seat and the other kids followed when they realised they hadn't won. Eloise had, and I knew her well. We went to primary school together. Her bright red hair was recognisable from a mile away. I scanned the classroom windows and saw her two doors up from Marla.

Eloise was dancing on her seat. She jumped up and down with her phone held aloft. Half her class were clapping and laughing despite the teacher's desperate attempts to calm them down. Eloise waved her phone back and forth above her head. The excitable students gathered around her desk. The other half stayed in their seats and didn't flinch.

In my class, Ms Orbison had started to teach again. She was still explaining how to solve equations, but I wasn't listening. I was watching Eloise's class as they willed her on. Their teacher had completely given up and was sitting back in his seat with his eyes shut as the kids chanted and danced.

I couldn't hear what they were saying, but I assumed they wanted Eloise to claim her prize. She held out her phone and the masses held their breath. The smile on Eloise's face was wide enough for me to see it clearly from across the school. She looked at her phone and tapped the screen.

For a second, she waited. The onlookers clasped their hands together and bit their lips but, as she looked at the image, Eloise's smile faded. In fact, it didn't just fade, it was wiped away completely.

CHAPTER TWELVE

ELOISE WAS NO longer happy, but she wasn't sad either. She was nothing. Her face showed no emotion. Her arms fell to the side and she sat neatly back down into her chair, even as the other kids huddled in a circle and waited eagerly to know what she'd won.

I furrowed my brow and leaned closer. Something wasn't right. Eloise had stopped smiling as soon as she claimed her prize. The kids were losing interest and the teacher finally managed to corral them back to their seats, but I kept watching from across the school.

Eloise didn't move. Her arms were flat on the table and her eyes never left the teacher as he started to speak at the front of the class. She went from ecstasy to apathy in the blink of an eye, from happiness to nothingness. From free will to under control.

My heart beat more firmly in my chest. Beads of sweat broke out on my forehead. Something wasn't right. More and more kids were acting like robots. I scratched my head and rubbed my jaw. Then, the phones buzzed again. They were becoming more frequent.

Once more, half the students stayed perfectly still while the other half raced to tap their screens. Ms Orbison sighed and sat back in her chair. She rubbed her eyes and yawned as Gus Martoni burst into celebration.

He punched the air and bit his lip with satisfaction while warning everyone else to stay away. He'd won the race and earned his prize. He wasn't going to let anyone else take it from him. He moved to the back of the room and shielded his phone like it was a flame in the wind. His mouth was slack as he tapped the screen once more. Flashing lights reflected in his wide eyes but, as he claimed his reward, his expression changed.

Just like Eloise, Gus's emotion drained from his face in an instant. His arms dropped, his mouth straightened. He wasn't happy and he wasn't sad. All humanity left his body and he walked mechanically back to his seat a shell of his previous self.

My jaw dropped. My face flushed red. It all started to dawn on me. Matt Jenkins was the first to go. He changed immediately after becoming a Buzztap champion. He'd also become a shadow of his former self, he had no emotion, no feelings, no mind of his own. Then, Callum Minks won and he changed too. Now, Eloise and Gus. Buzztap had to be the cause. It was the link between them all. It wasn't just a game. It was something so much worse.

CHAPTER THIRTEEN

"THE APP..." I mumbled. "It's *controlling* their *minds*."

"Huh?" the kid next to me asked.

"Buzztap!" I said, louder this time. "Look what it's doing. They've been stripped of their personalities. It's like they've been drugged!"

"Toby," Ms Orbison called. "Pipe down back there."

"They've been brainwashed!"

"I mean it, Toby," she warned. "I've had enough today, one more peep out of you and you'll be in detention for the rest of the week."

I paused. I wanted to speak, but I didn't dare. I couldn't risk getting detention. I'd been in trouble too much this year already, my parents would ground me for a century. I bit my lip and sat back in my chair. My knee bobbed up and down as I tapped my foot. I sighed deeply and scratched my neck. It was so obvious now. All the kids sitting with their arms on the tables and with vacant expressions in their eyes had been brainwashed. They'd all won the Buzztap game and they were all under the control of something or someone.

I had to tell Marla. She was obsessed with Buzztap. Like everyone else in school, it seemed to have taken over her life. It was only me and the teachers that didn't, or couldn't, play it. Marla loved the game and was determined to win at some point. When she did, she'd become just like the others. The entire school would be the same. No personalities, no laughter. Just robotic people obeying every order they're given without thinking or questioning.

I was looking into Marla's classroom when the bell rang. I leapt from my seat and headed towards the door. The route was clear because half the class wouldn't move until Ms Orbison instructed them to. I skipped through the remaining kids and slipped through the door before anyone could stop me. I had to get to Marla before the phones buzzed again.

I was halfway down the corridor when the brainwashed kids started to move. All at once, every robotic student slid their chair back in exactly the same way and pushed it into place at the exact same time. They moved as one. Every classroom in every hall. They filtered out of the doors and flooded into the open spaces like ants exiting an anthill.

The game must have been running much more frequently than I realised because it seemed like half the school had already been brainwashed. The unaffected kids were easy to spot. They were the only ones walking with bad posture and not marching in unison.

I was crossing the central courtyard when the phones buzzed again. Kids in every corner reached for their devices. They dropped their bags and stopped walking. Pens and pencils scattered across the cold, stone floor.

I froze. All I could do was wait. One more person was going to get stripped of their entire personality. One more person was going to become a robotic zombie and join the hoard. All around me, people frowned and grimaced as they realised they hadn't been quick enough this time, unaware of what would happen to them if they had. One girl was picking up her pencils as I approached.

"Who was it?" I asked. "Who won?"

'Huh?" she grunted. "Oh, I don't know, some girl named Mandy, I think."

"Mandy?" I repeated. "Are you sure?"

"Something like that," she shrugged. "Here, look for yourself."

I took the phone and swiped right to the scoreboard. My throat ran dry. My hands shook. The name at the top wasn't Mandy.

It was Marla.

CHAPTER FOURTEEN

I BLINKED ONCE and only once. I didn't have time to waste. I had to find my friend before she claimed her prize. I threw the phone into the air, turned and ran. I heard the girl call me a nasty name as she caught it, but I was already sprinting towards the double doors. Marla's last class was on the third floor, but I hoped she wasn't still there. I hoped she had started walking down the stairs and I'd bump into her before she had time to look at her prize.

I bashed my way through the crowd and into the building. The air was stale and the hallway reeked of body odour and old books. I scanned the faces as I squeezed in between the kids as they filed out in an immaculately organised queue. They didn't even look at me when I barged my shoulder against theirs. I was nothing to them. They just kept marching, straight-faced and emotionless.

There must've been even more winners than I thought because the flow of zombie robots kept coming. They snaked up the stairs and down each hallway. The school was packed with kids, but it was eerily quiet as no one spoke. They just kept marching in silence, one after the other. Hundreds of the emotionless drones passed by as I kept running. I scanned their faces in the hope I wouldn't see Marla.

The third floor was less busy. The last of the brainwashed army had left and the hallway felt wide and open in comparison. I slowed to a walk. My chest thumped. My legs burned. I panted as I approached Marla's class. The door swung open and I stepped inside.

"Marla!" She was in the corner with her back to me. Her head was down and her phone was in her hands. "Don't look at it, Marla! It will turn you into one of them!"

My hip knocked a desk and sent a pot of pens flying as I raced across the room. It was just me and her. Everyone else had left. I turned sideways and edged between tables as quickly as I could. Marla's face lifted from her phone. I could only see the back of her head as I called her name again and again.

She didn't answer. My breath was weak and my voice was low. I reached out a hand and squeezed her shoulder. Her hip swivelled. Her neck turned. Her cold, soulless eyes stared straight through me.

CHAPTER FIFTEEN

"MARLA?" I MUMBLED, trying to hold back the tears. "Are you there?" There was no answer. Marla's face was straight. Her mouth was closed and her eyes were dull. She stared at the wall behind me as I grabbed her shoulders and shook. "ANSWER ME!" I screamed, but there was still no response.

Marla's brain had been fried like all the others. Her body was just a shell with no personality of her own. I slumped back, perched on the table behind me and watched her walk towards the door. She moved only in straight lines. Her back was completely straight and her head faced forwards at all times. When she got to the end of the row, she stopped and turned 90 degrees before starting to move again like a soldier on a march.

My jaw was wide open as I struggled to understand what I was seeing. I scratched my head and exhaled deeply. Marla's eyes scared me. Normally they were bright and attentive, now they were dull and dark. It was like she didn't recognise me at all or, if she did, she just didn't care. I didn't know which was worse.

I stood up straight and headed back through the empty classroom. Almost all of the chairs were tucked neatly under the desks. Usually, the classrooms were a mess after students left. The hallway was deserted, but from the window at the end, I could see into the courtyard below. Hundreds of kids lined up in rows of four. They marched together, snaking all around the school. There were so many of them that I couldn't see the other end.

Marla's black hair barely moved as she walked. She left the double doors and strode across the school to join the back of the queue. No one laughed or smiled. They all just marched together like pre-programmed robots.

I trudged slowly down the stairs. It was break time, but I didn't know what to do. Normally, I'd hang out with Marla and we'd make jokes and share our lunches. I watched her march with the others and disappear around the corner. I had no idea what they were doing or where they were going.

The courtyard was almost empty after the brainwashed people left, but there were still a few normal kids left in the corners. I looked down at them as they shook their heads and pointed at the others. Suddenly, they all reached into their pockets and yanked out their phones. Buzztap had started again.

They bashed their screens as they raced to be first. They had no idea. They were completely oblivious to what they were walking into. I thumped the window and shouted for them to stop, but they couldn't hear me.

I ran down the stairs two at a time. I spun around the corners and leapt down each flight as quickly as I possibly could. Through the window, I saw a boy to the left with his arms raised in celebration. I had to stop him before he claimed his prize. I ran quicker and skipped down more steps but, at the next window, someone else raised their arms too.

I was almost at the bottom so I kept going and barged through the double doors. By the time my eyes adjusted to the sunlight bursting through the clouds, three more kids were jumping up and down in celebration.

I picked one and ran towards him, but it was too late. His expression changed as soon as he looked at his phone. His arms fell to his side and his back straightened. I knew what was happening, I didn't have time to watch him march away. I had to try to save the others. Buzztap was crowning more than one winner at a time. I ran to the other side of the courtyard, but I was too slow. They'd already turned. All of them. Half a dozen kids looked straight through me and started to march. They had all looked at the prize. I grabbed handfuls of their clothing but they shrugged me off and kept going until I was the only one left.

The entire courtyard was empty. I'd never seen it without people before. Normally, it was the loudest place in the school but now it was deserted. I tried to find someone else, but I couldn't. There was no one there. My only choice was to follow the crowd so I ran in the direction the kids had gone.

Every classroom I passed was empty. The chairs were neatly stored under the tables and the books were stacked in organised piles. Even the canteen was deserted. The school was a ghost town.

I jogged through the grounds to find the students. They hadn't gone far, but I was still surprised to see them. The main playground was large, and they filled every centimetre. Students and teachers stood side by side, arms straight, legs rigid. They were evenly spaced and stared straight ahead with their backs to me.

I took a slow step forwards. Hundreds of people faced away from me. It must've been everyone in the school. I could even see the headteacher towards the middle, standing perfectly still like everyone else. It was so quiet I could hear myself breathing.

"Hello Toby," a shrill voice whispered from behind me. I jumped and spun on the spot to see Mr Simon standing over me with a phone in his hand.

"Sir!" I gasped. "You have to help me, I don't know what's going on. It's like everyone's been brainwashed!"

"Beautiful, isn't it?"

"Yeah… wait. *What?*"

"No more chatting. No more misbehaving. Just the perfect kids studying in the perfect school."

"Mr Simon… What have you done?"

"I've done what I should've done a long time ago," he said, waving his phone in the air. "I've made *changes.*"

"It was you," I gasped. "You created the app? You created Buzztap?"

"Exactly!" Mr Simon said. His thin, grey lips parted as he grinned widely.

"But why?"

"Do you really need to ask? Look at them. They're *perfect.*"

"But they're not themselves anymore! You've taken their personalities. You've taken their identities. You've taken everything from them!"

"Brilliant, right?" Mr Simon shrugged. "But there's just one more problem I need to solve…" His dull eyes grew narrower and his smile faded. "Something wrong with your phone, Toby?"

"It broke," I muttered. "I haven't bought a new one yet."

"Hmm, I thought as much. That's a real pity."

"A pity?"

"If I can't control your mind," Mr Simon sneered. "I'll have to make you disappear completely."

Mr Simon drew his boney finger up in front of his face and tapped it lightly against the screen of his phone. A thousand shoes stomped to the floor behind me. I spun around and felt my breath shoot from my body. Every single student and teacher had turned on the spot and was staring right at me with their fists clenched.

"Please, Sir," I begged. "Let me go."

"It's far too late for that, Toby. Far, far too late."

CHAPTER SIXTEEN

WITH ANOTHER TAP on his phone, Mr Simon's brainwashed army raised their arms and advanced. They moved together as if connected by an invisible string. Their legs swept up and down at the same speed and their feet slammed into the ground at the exact same time.

I raised my shaking hands in front of my face as I backed away. My knees were weak and my heart pounded in my chest. A high-pitched wail squeezed from my dry, harsh throat as the entire school marched towards me.

Their eyes were dull but focused. Their arms stretched out towards me and their fingers clenched and unclenched as if preparing to wring my neck. Their heads tilted forwards and their dead eyes glinted in the sun. I backed up further until I bumped into Mr Simon.

"Careful, boy," he sneered, holding his phone up high. "You almost made me drop it."

"What's happening?" I asked. "What are they doing?"

"It's simple," Mr Simon said. "They're going to kill you." A frozen chill ran across my skin and Mr Simon's words echoed around my brain. "Unless, of course," he continued. "You start behaving."

"Behaving? I'll behave, I promise! Call them off!"

"It's not as simple as that," Mr Simon chuckled as the brainwashed students stomped ever nearer. "I don't want promises. I want your mind. Look at my phone and this will all be over."

"If I look at your phone, I'll be just like them!"

"Exactly."

"I won't do it!" I screamed. "I refuse. You can't make me."

"You're right, *I* can't make you," Mr Simon said, calmly. "But, *they* can."

I turned back to face the mass of soulless, brainwashed students as their walk turned into a jog and their jog turned into a run.

CHAPTER SEVENTEEN

I SCREAMED AS I stumbled past Mr Simon and staggered away. The students sprinted at full speed. Their faces were unchanged, but their bodies were working hard. Their dead expressions remained neutral as their arms and legs pumped furiously and they charged towards me.

There was no time to think. I had to run. I twisted on one foot and took off back towards the courtyard. The sound of a thousand footsteps on hard concrete echoed around the school as I skipped around the corner as quickly as I could.

The students weren't far behind. I turned and looked over my shoulder as they came around the bend. Their backs were straight and their arms were bent at the elbow. Each kid was exactly the same. They weren't as fast as me, but they didn't look like stopping.

My breath was already running low. My lungs were tight and I paused for a second to suck in more oxygen. The students were still in lines of four. They turned the corner in perfect formation like fighter jets banking around a steep bend.

I couldn't waste more time catching my breath. I turned and ran through the pair of double doors that led to a staircase in the main teaching block. The classrooms were still empty and my clumsy footsteps pierced the silence.

I was on the second floor when the doors crashed open again. Glass shattered as the brainwashed students slammed them against the wall and rushed inside. I stopped for a second and peered down the gap between the stairs. The kids didn't even flinch as shards of glass rained down on top of them. They just kept running.

When I reached the top floor, my thighs felt like they were on fire, my knees were sore and my back ached. The sound of footsteps climbing quickly up the stairs behind me told me I couldn't rest for even a second. They didn't slow down. The footsteps were still the same, each one synchronised with the others.

I couldn't keep sprinting. I stumbled along the hallway, bracing myself against the lockers on either side as the students reached the top of the stairs. They didn't stop and they didn't hesitate. They weren't even out of breath. They just kept running towards me with their expressionless faces giving nothing away. Their arms pumped and their knees lifted up and down without skipping a beat.

I tried to jog, but a pain shot across my stomach. I pressed my hand to the stitch and kept moving. I hobbled forwards as the sound of the footsteps neared. I didn't dare look back. They were almost on top of me as I dragged myself further along the hallway.

The pain in my side stretched to my belly button and made it almost impossible to run normally. Every step I took was slower than the last. Every step more painful. I dragged my legs towards the end of the corridor, but I was running out of time and out of space.

The brainwashed army charged ever closer. I panted and grunted. I could see the staircase. If I could make it, maybe I could shake them off, but it was too late. They were too fast and they never slowed down. I reached the window at the end of the hall, but I couldn't reach the stairs.

The sound of their furious footsteps slamming against the dull carpet overwhelmed my senses. I stumbled towards the window and felt my fingers slide down the cold, wet glass. It was too late. They were too strong. Too fast. Too close.

CHAPTER EIGHTEEN

I TURNED AROUND and awaited my fate. I slumped against the window and felt the frigid condensation run down my neck as the students rushed towards me. They showed no emotion, no pain and no mercy. Their robotic arms swung back and forth as they closed the gap between us.

I sighed deeply and turned my head to the window. I didn't want to see them coming. The courtyard below was almost completely empty. Just one figure stood in the middle with a phone in his hand. Mr Simon. His eyes were peering towards me and both hands clasped his phone.

I was far away, but I could just make out his thumbs moving rapidly across the screen and the huge, vile grin stretched across his wrinkled face. He was laughing. He could see the soulless army charging towards me and he was enjoying every second of it. His boney shoulders bobbed up and down as he arched his back and roared with laughter.

I didn't have long to look at Mr Simon. Suddenly, all the air was pushed from my lungs as I was hit from the side. The brainwashed students had arrived. The force sent me sprawling to the ground. My vision blurred as I rolled over and instinctively scrambled to get away.

The floor was rough and hard. My knees scraped and my elbows bruised as I hurried across the thin carpet, but I wasn't quick enough. A foot connected with my ribs. A fist landed between my shoulder blades. A knee dug into my thigh. I rolled. I kicked. I lashed out in every direction as more bodies piled on top of me.

I found myself on my back. Dozens of kids were flooding through the doors. Their shoulders bumped into each other as the hallway narrowed. More and more piled on top of me. Their faces were impassive. Unflinching. Robotic. I forced my knees up towards my chest and felt the crushing weight of several bodies weighing them down. I pushed a chest and hit an elbow. Fists flew by my face as I kept them at an arm's length, but my strength wouldn't hold out for long.

I had to move. I felt something hard behind my head and clenched my hand around the metal railing of the staircase. I pulled with all my might. My back slid across the rough floor and freed my knees just enough to be able to twist and turn my body. A hand scraped by my face as Callum Minks took a swipe. My foot sprung free. I kicked out and sent Callum flying backwards into a pile of other bodies that ricocheted like bowling pins.

For a fraction of a second, I had space to move. I lifted myself up and darted towards the stairs. A foot swiped by my ankles but I leapt down the steps just in time. The brainwashed students tripped over themselves as they surged towards me, but it didn't stop them for long. I bounded down the stairs two at a time. I could barely breathe. White-hot pain shot through my knees with every step I took. My mind raced in a blind panic and I hurtled away from the silent mob as quickly as I could. Everything was a blur, but I knew I couldn't stop moving.

I crashed through another set of double doors and stumbled out into the sunlight. The students were close behind. Their footsteps rumbled down the last of the stairs. They were no longer disorganised. They were running in perfect formation again, arms pumping in unison and faces as expressionless as ever.

Further in the courtyard, Mr Simon stood with his phone in his hands and a sinister smirk still plastered across his face. I slowed to a walk. The students bashed the door behind me and sent shards of glass flying, but I didn't run, because I knew exactly what I had to do.

CHAPTER NINETEEN

I APPROACHED SLOWLY and Mr Simon stared menacingly. His small, dark eyes sparkled with joy as his brainwashed army did his bidding. I could hear them approaching behind me. Closer and closer. Their feet slapped against the pavement and the sound grew louder, but I didn't react.

Mr Simon directed them towards me with another tap of his phone. I stopped walking and held my breath. They were within striking distance. I shut my eyes and waited for the blow, but it never came.

I opened my eyes again and turned around. The students were frozen mid-stride. Their expressions were blank, but their arms were raised. Their fists were clenched. Knees up. They had stopped less than a second from hitting my back. I turned to Mr Simon.

"Ready to accept your fate?" he smirked, holding the phone aloft for me to see. "One more tap and they'll tear you limb from limb."

"I'm ready," I sighed and took a step forwards.

"After you watch this video, you'll be mine forever. No more thinking. No more opinions and no more disobedience. You'll never smile again. Never laugh. You'll come to school, do your work in silence then go home and do your homework in silence until I let you sleep. You'll do this every day for the rest of your life. Got it?"

"Got it," I nodded, exhaling deeply. "Let's get it over with."

Mr Simon hopped from one foot to the other. He was giddy with excitement. A fleck of saliva gathered at the corner of his thin lips as he shuffled towards me.

"Now," he chuckled. "Just look at the screen and it will all be over before you know it. No more thoughts. No more nothing. Just education."

I swallowed hard and took a deep breath. Mr Simon's boney arm stretched out between us. The students were frozen in time behind me, awaiting their instructions. I turned slightly to let Mr Simon get closer. He held his phone up and checked the screen one last time. His tongue peeked out the corner of his mouth as he concentrated on pressing the right buttons.

"Come on," I muttered.

"Alright, alright, keep your hair on," Mr Simon said. "Here, look at this and it will all be over."

Mr Simon stopped about a metre in front of me and held the phone up for me to look at.

"I can't see," I lied, looking past the phone and into the teacher's eyes. "It's too far away."

"And you kids think *my* eyes are bad!" Mr Simon quipped. "How about now?"

"A bit closer," I urged. "I lost my glasses in the fight."

I gestured to a graze on my arm. Mr Simon sighed but accepted my excuse. He took another step towards me and it was all I needed. I lunged forwards, grabbed the phone and, before he even knew what was happening, took off running.

CHAPTER TWENTY

I SPRINTED AS fast as I could while smashing the *back* button with my thumb. Mr Simon started to chase me but quickly realised it was no use. I was faster and fitter than him. We both knew he'd never catch me.

I took a deep breath before looking at the phone. My gamble paid off. There was nothing left on the screen to brainwash me after I'd mashed the buttons. Instead, there were four arrows and a few other options. I looked up from the screen to see Mr Simon frozen in time like the students behind him. Except, he hadn't been made to stop, he was just scared. His outstretched arm reached across the gap between us as my fingers hovered over the screen.

I pointed the phone at the students and tapped the buttons. In an instant, they snapped their heels together and fell into line to await their next order. I tapped the left arrow and they marched to the side. I pressed pause and they stopped. They were under my full control. I could make them do anything I wanted.

I instructed them to march forwards, then back. I made them turn in a circle, jump into the air and clap their hands and then, finally, I made them surround Mr Simon completely. Hundreds of students joined the group and they filled the space around us.

"Turn them back," I barked. "Turn them back to normal or I'll make them attack."

"Please," the teacher whimpered. "Order them to stop."

"No way," I said, shaking my head and pressing the button to make the brainwashed army close tighter in on their target. "Turn them back right now!" The students marched closer and the circle constricted like a noose.

"Please!" Mr Simon cried.

"This is your last chance," I said, calmly. "You have 5 seconds. 5… 4…"

"Wait!"

"3."

"Stop!"

"2."

"I'll do it, I'll do it!" Mr Simon said, finally. "You just have to promise me one thing."

"What's that?" I replied.

"Promise me you'll die quietly."

"Me?" I choked. "You really think you're in a position to be making those sort of comments?"

I raised the phone and pressed the button to advance, but nothing happened.

"Funny, isn't it?" Mr Simon continued, straightening his back and standing taller than before. "You kids always underestimate us."

"Wait," I squeaked. "Why isn't it working?"

"You really think I would allow third-party access to *my* app?"

I shook the phone and looked at the screen. A message appeared.

"Access denied. Enter admin password."

Slowly, I realised what was happening. My eyes grew wider. A bead of sweat burst from my forehead. My throat felt dry and rough as I swallowed heavily. Mr Simon stepped forwards and barged easily through the refrozen students.

"Did it ever occur to you that I might have planned for this?" he growled. "Are you really so arrogant to think I would make it that easy for you?"

My arm fell limp. The phone slipped from my fingers and crashed to the floor. I stepped back as the students turned. Their cold, emotionless faces locked onto mine as Mr Simon pulled another phone from his back pocket and controlled them again.

CHAPTER TWENTY-ONE

"NO," I MUMBLED. "This can't be happening."
Marla's face appeared from the crowd. She was one
of them. On her left, Callum Minks. On her right,
Matt Jenkins. Together, they marched towards me.
"Marla, please. It's me. It's Toby."

Marla didn't listen. She *couldn't* listen. She
moved towards me with cold, unseeing eyes. Her
arms swung in time with the others. Her feet stamped
to the same beat.

I backed away, slowly at first. Mr Simon's smirk
turned into a grin as he tapped furiously on his new
phone. The army's pace increased. Their legs moved
further. Their arms swung faster. They broke into a
run, and so did I.

My heart felt like it was about to burst through my
chest. I didn't know what to do but run. Everything
around me turned into a blur as I sprinted through the
school. A thousand robotic feet thumped into the
ground as the students gave chase.

I entered buildings, clambered up stairs and ran
through hallways. The school seemed bigger without

kids loitering in the halls. The corridors were empty and they echoed loudly as I slammed the doors back on their hinges and fled in any direction I could.

The wave of footsteps flooded in behind me wherever I went. I couldn't outrun them forever. They never tired. Never stopped. Everywhere I went, they followed. A thousand blank faces around every corner.

I jumped through the frame of a door the brainless army had smashed to smithereens and stumbled back out into the sunlight. I didn't have long. I could hear them clattering down the stairs. I needed help. I patted my pockets for my phone before remembering I didn't have it. I was all alone. I had to get out. I had to get away.

The only exit was on the other side of the school. It was my only chance. I coughed and spluttered as I dragged myself across the courtyard. My legs were heavy and my chest was tight.

Mr Simon was still orchestrating the attack from his phone. Two large students from the year above stood on either side of him as he controlled the army from afar. His guards were much larger than me. They didn't blink and didn't move. I wouldn't have stood a chance against them.

The rest of the students poured into the courtyard. Marla, Matt and Callum were at the front of the pack. They surged towards me again as I turned and ran. My breath had barely returned, but I couldn't wait any longer.

Marla swiped an arm, but I ducked out of the way. Callum kicked my shins, but I kept my footing. Matt reached for my throat, but missed by a millimetre.

They were right behind me as I ran through the school. I was too tired to sprint faster. My legs wouldn't carry me much further.

The doors to the street came into view as I spun around a wide corner. They were large, black and open. The faintest smile spread across my lips as the exit grew closer. I could almost reach out and grab the handle, but then it all faded.

Dozens of school shoes stamped down between me and the outside world. More brainwashed students filed into the space and completely cut off my path to safety. I turned to the right, but more kids appeared in a doorway. To my left, more again. Everywhere I looked, I saw brainwashed kids.

I was completely surrounded.

CHAPTER TWENTY-TWO

MARLA LUNGED. I dropped to the floor and felt her fall over my head as Callum came charging in behind. I rolled over and sprang to my feet just in time to evade his outstretched arms. Matt threw a punch. It cuffed my shoulder and sent me spiralling to the side as the others closed in.

I hit the ground hard and found myself eye-level with a forest of shins as the mass of bodies closed the circle around me. Out the corner of my vision, I saw something. A branch. It hung low over the gap we used to get to the pond.

I had no time to think, I had to make a break for it. I scrambled to my feet and dived for the bush. Fingers scraped my sides as I flew through the air. Bodies lunged. Mr Simon yelled in the distance.

Branches scratched my cheeks as I broke through the bushes and towards the pond on the other side. My elbows hit the muddy bank and I rolled over and tumbled to the bottom without stopping. The students rushed through the tiny gap behind me. I saw glimpses of their expressionless faces every time I flipped onto my back.

Covered in mud, I came to a stop on the bank and stared up at the army piling through the gap. They ran down the hill with straight backs and pumping arms. Over my shoulder, I could see the rope hanging limply over the dark water. I had no time to waste.

I bounced to my feet and rushed towards the edge of the pond. The rope was stationary. The water was still. The students clattered towards me and raised their fists as I jumped. I felt the wind brush past my shoulders and outstretched hands swipe at my back.

I flew through the air as the brainwashed army leapt from the bank. My eyes strained in their sockets as my fingers reached for the swing. It burned the skin on my palm as I closed my hand tightly around it. The rope dug into my fingers as it took my full weight and my momentum propelled me forwards.

Water rained down onto the back of my head as the students crashed into the pond behind me. The far side of the bank approached quickly and I let go just in time. My body sailed perfectly through the air and I landed with a heavy *thud* into the mud and brambles on the other side.

I turned onto my side and watched the army as they kept coming. Many had fallen into the water as they dived to reach me, but others were still on the bank. They tried to stop themselves from falling too, but there were too many of them. There wasn't any space, but they kept piling through the gap in the hedge. The whole school filed in and forced the ones at the front into the pond. *Splash* after *splash* after *splash*.

Marla was in the water. She must've been closest to me as I jumped, but something was different about her. Her face wasn't passive. Her eyebrows were furrowed and her nose was wrinkled. She looked around in disgust and confusion as if she had just woken up.

I reached out my hand and pulled her onto the bank next to me. She was dazed and confused, but she wasn't murderous. She was no longer trying to hurt me.

"W… what happened?" she asked, pulling her wet hair from her face. "Where am I?"

Another pair of hands slapped onto the bank before I could answer and Matt Jenkins pulled himself up.

"Why were we in the pond?" he coughed. "What happened to our lesson with Mr Simon?"

"My phone!" Callum Minks yelled from the other bank. "It's completely busted!"

"That's it!" I realised. "Your phones have been fried like mine. He can't control you anymore."

"Who can't?" Marla asked, but her question was answered by Mr Simon as he came sliding down the bank on the far side.

"What are you doing?" he growled while furiously slamming buttons on his phone. "I ordered you to attack him!"

As the crowd of students climbed out of the pond and gained their bearings, they started to realise what had happened.

"It was him!" I called. "He brainwashed all of you!"

A hundred dripping-wet faces turned to Mr Simon and a slow realisation dawned.

"I remember now…" one said.

"You made us do all those things!" another chirped.

"Get him!" a third screamed.

Mr Simon's expression was far from blank. His jaw dropped. His eyebrows raised. His phone fell from his trembling hands and slid into the pond below. He turned and ran as dozens of furious kids chased him back through the gap in the hedge and out of sight.

The teacher's hoarse voice faded and was replaced by silence as we were left alone. Marla's dark eyes twinkled as pond water ran down her cheeks. She turned her sodden phone over in her hands, looked up at me and smiled.

"You did it, then?" she said, nodding to the thick rope swaying gently in the breeze.

"Yep," I chuckled. "I told you it'd be awesome."

The next few days were strangely quiet. Not as quiet as when the whole school was brainwashed, of course, but most of the kids took a while to get back to their normal selves. Apart from Matt Jenkins, that is. He immediately resumed his role as the class clown. I'd *almost* missed him.

No one spoke about what happened. Most people shrugged and feigned ignorance when it was brought up, but I suspected they remembered more than they would let on. It was just easier to ignore it and move on, so that's exactly what we did.

On the rare occasions when people did speak about it, some said Mr Simon kept running forever. Others said he was arrested and thrown in prison. A few kids even claimed he now works for the government on top-secret mind-control projects. All I know is, we never saw Mr Simon again.

It was a week later when my new phone arrived. It was sitting on the doormat when I got home. I unwrapped it eagerly and turned it on as soon as possible. It had been quite nice not having a phone, not to mention it literally saved my life, but I was excited to have one again so I could start chatting with my friends.

It powered up and buzzed into life as I heard laughter and shouting from the other room. Mum was cheering. Dad was giggling. I slipped through the door with my new phone in hand.

"What's up?" I asked. "What's going on?"

"It's this new app," Dad chuckled.

"You should try it," Mum added.

"What's it called?"

"Tapbuzz!" they yelled together.

More SCARETOWN books available now.

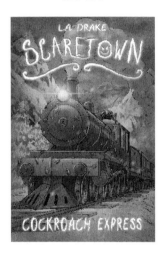

Elliot and Archie are step-brothers forced together on a family holiday. Their parents hope they'll bond, but their relaxing week away doesn't quite go as planned when they discover not everything on the train is as normal as it first appears.

Now, they need to put their differences aside to escape the monsters that lurk onboard the COCKROACH EXPRESS.

AVAILABLE TO READ NOW. FIND OUT MORE AT WWW.SCARETOWNBOOKS.COM

More SCARETOWN books available now.

Flick, Izzy and Zach think they've found the perfect place to hang out. It's quiet, cool and secluded. But when strange things start happening, they realise they're not alone in Clown Cemetery.

Now, they must fight against the inhabitants whose slumber they've unwittingly disturbed.

CLOWN CEMETERY is another thrill ride for kids everywhere who love the SCARETOWN series.

AVAILABLE TO READ NOW. FIND OUT MORE AT WWW.SCARETOWNBOOKS.COM

CLOWN CEMETERY

1.

"Get back here," they called. Their voices were hoarse and sharp. Their breath laboured under the strain of pushing the pedals. Two of them were chasing me, but I was quick. I stamped down hard and felt my bike surge forwards. My knuckles gripped the tough rubber handlebars and I held on tight as I skidded around the corner.

I clenched the fingers on my left hand and the back brake clamped onto the rim of the wheel. Dirt and dust sprayed into the air as my thin tyre screeched across the concrete. I turned the handlebars and pointed the front end towards the corner. I couldn't look, but I could sense them close behind. I could hear their chests wheezing as they hurried towards me.

I couldn't stop. They were too close. One false move and they'd be on me. I leaned forwards and forced my feet downwards, one after the other. The bike straightened itself as I accelerated out of the corner and sped along the road.

Houses whizzed past on either side. I was a long way from home. I'd never been on that side of town before. A curtain twitched. A door slammed shut. I kept peddling even though my legs were burning and my chest was tight.

I raised my head and gasped for air. The cold oxygen rushed down my throat and spread through my lungs. I swallowed hard and hunched low over the handlebars. I had to keep going. The gap between us was closing.

They were right behind me. I gritted my teeth and glanced over my shoulder. They weren't slowing down. I had to do something. I had to think of a way out. I scanned the buildings in the distance as my legs turned the pedals as quickly as they could.

I reached up and brushed a stream of sweat from my eyes. The bike swerved slightly to the left but I caught it just in time. The line of houses continued far into the distance. I knew I wouldn't be able to last long enough to get to the end.

I glanced left and right. There had to be somewhere I could go. Every house looked the same. Every door and every window was identical. Even the cars were similar. On the road to my right, other vehicles zoomed by. I couldn't flag them down, I was moving too fast and I couldn't stop for even a second.

A lorry thundered past. Gravel and dust splattered my face. I scrunched my eyes shut until it passed. When I opened them again, I saw something. On the other side of the street, there was an opening. It was small but it was just wide enough to fit through. I couldn't slow down and I couldn't wait. I had to go immediately. I checked over my shoulder, saw a break in the traffic and went for it.

I thudded down from the kerb and burst across the road. The path on the other side was made of gravel and my front tyre sunk between the stones, but I kept going. A large tree almost completely blocked the entrance. Its soft, floppy leaves brushed my head as I powered through the undergrowth and darted between the gap in the wall.

For a second, the sunlight was completely blocked and everything was dark. My vision returned a fraction too late to see it coming. In front of me, a large hole in the ground came into view as I sped towards it. I yanked my handlebars to the side but it wasn't enough. The angle was too sharp. My bike jutted to the left and I went to the right as the tyre dug into the soft ground and threw me off.

I flew through the air and crashed back down with a *thud.* My elbows and knees scraped the earth as I rolled across the surface. Mud kicked up into the air and I could smell the wet grass as it brushed against my cheek. For a second, everything was blurry.

Then I saw them. The two people that had been chasing me. They rolled to a controlled stop, climbed slowly from their bikes and took a step closer. The larger one cracked his knuckles. The smaller one smirked.

My fingers dug into the ground and my heart thumped against my chest as they advanced. I had nowhere to go. Nowhere to run. Nowhere to hide.

CLOWN CEMETERY is available now in digital or paperback. Visit www.scaretownbooks.com for more information.

Join the conversation at www.twitter.com/scaretownbooks